Contents

Round and Round the Garden

Round and round the garden
Like a teddy bear;
One step, two step,
Tickle you under there!

Georgie Porgie

Georgie Porgie, pudding and pie,
Kissed the girls and made them cry;
When the boys came out to play,
Georgie Porgie ran away.

A Cat came Fiddling

A cat came fiddling out of a barn,
With a pair of bagpipes under her arm.
She could sing nothing but fiddle dee dee,
The mouse has married the bumblebee.
Pipe, cat; dance, mouse;
We'll have a wedding
at our good house.

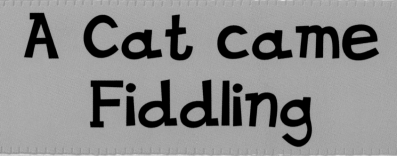

Goldilocks and the Three Bears

A retelling from the original tale
by Andrew Lang

Once upon a time there was a little girl called Goldilocks who lived in the middle of a great forest with her mother and father. Now ever since she was tiny, her mother had told her she must never, ever wander off into the forest for it was full of wild creatures, especially bears. But as

Goldilocks grew older she longed to explore the forest.

One washday, when her mother was busy in the kitchen, hidden in clouds of steam, Goldilocks sneaked off down the path that led deep into the forest. At first she was happy, looking at the wild flowers and

listening to the birds singing, but it did not take long for her to become hopelessly lost.

She wandered for hours and hours and, as it grew darker, she became frightened. She started to cry, but then she saw a light shining through the trees. She rushed forward, sure she had found her way home, only to realize that it was not her own cottage that she was looking at. Even so, she opened the door and looked inside.

On a scrubbed wooden table there were three bowls of steaming hot porridge – a big one, a middle-sized one and a little one. Goldilocks was so tired that she quite forgot all her manners and just sat down at the table. The big bowl was too tall for her to

reach. The middle-sized bowl was too hot.
But the little one was just right, so she ate
all the porridge up.

By the warm fire there were three
chairs – a big one, a middle-sized one and a
little one. Goldilocks couldn't climb up onto
the big one. The middle-sized one was too
hard. The little one was just the right size,

but as soon as she sat down, it broke into
pieces. Goldilocks scrambled to her feet and
then noticed there were steps going upstairs,
where she found three beds – a big one, a
middle-sized one and a little one. The big

bed was too hard. The middle-sized one was too soft. But the little one was just right and she was soon fast asleep.

The cottage belonged to three bears, and it was not long before they came home. They knew immediately that someone had been inside.

Father Bear growled, "Who has been eating my porridge?"

Mother Bear grumbled, "Who has been eating my porridge?"

And Baby Bear gasped, "Who has been eating my porridge, AND has eaten it all up?"

The bears looked around the room. They looked at the chairs by the warm fire.

Father Bear growled, "Who has been sitting on my chair?"

Mother Bear grumbled, "Who has been sitting on my chair?"

And Baby Bear gasped, "Who has been sitting on my chair, AND has broken it to bits?"

The bears went upstairs to take a look at their beds.

Father Bear growled, "Who has been sleeping in my bed?"

Mother Bear grumbled, "Who has been sleeping in my bed?"

And Baby Bear gasped, "Who has been sleeping in my bed, AND is still there?"

Suddenly Goldilocks woke up. All she could see was three very cross-looking bears. She jumped off the bed, ran down the stairs, and out of the door. She ran and ran and ran, and by good fortune found herself outside her own cottage. Her mother and father scolded her, but then gave her lots of hugs and kisses, and a big bowl of soup. Goldilocks had certainly learnt her lesson, and she never ever wandered off again.

If all the Seas were One Sea

If all the seas were one sea,
What a great sea that would be!
If all the trees were one tree,
What a great tree that would be!
If all the axes were one axe,
What a great axe that would be!

And if all the men were one man,
What a great man that would be!
And if the great man took the great axe
And cut down the great tree
And let it fall into the great sea,
What a splish-splash that would be!

The Owl and the Pussy-cat

The Owl and the Pussy-cat went to sea
In a beautiful pea-green boat,
They took some honey,
and plenty of money,
Wrapped up in a five-pound note.

The Owl looked up to the stars above,
And sang to a small guitar,
"O lovely Pussy! O Pussy, my love,
What a beautiful Pussy you are,
you are, you are!
What a beautiful Pussy you are!"

Pussy said to the Owl, "You elegant fowl!
How charmingly sweet you sing!
O let us be married!
Too long have we tarried:
But what shall we do for a ring?"

They sailed away, for a year and a day,
To the land where the Bong-tree grows
And there in a wood a Piggy-wig stood
With a ring at the end of his nose,
his nose, his nose,
With a ring at the end of his nose.

"Dear Pig, are you willing to sell
for one shilling your ring?"
Said the Piggy, "I will."
So they took it away, and were
married next day
By the Turkey who lives on the hill.

They dined on mince, and slices of quince,
Which they ate with a runcible spoon;
And hand in hand, on the edge of the sand,
They danced by the light of the moon,
the moon, the moon,
They danced by the light of the moon.

Edward Lear
1812–88, b. England

Baa Baa
Black Sheep

Baa baa black sheep,
Have you any wool?
Yes, sir, yes, sir,
Three bags full;
One for my master,
One for my dame,
And one for the little boy
Who lives down the lane.

The Lion and the Unicorn

The Lion and the Unicorn
Were fighting for the crown;
The Lion beat the Unicorn
All about the town.

Some gave them white bread
And some gave them brown;
Some gave them plum cake
And drummed them out of town!

It's Raining

It's raining, it's pouring,
The old man is snoring,
He went to bed and
Bumped his head,
And couldn't get up
In the morning.

The Princess and the Pea

A retelling from the original story
by Hans Christian Andersen

The prince was very fed up. Everyone in the court, from his father, the king, down to the smallest paige, seemed to think it was time he was married. Now the prince would have been very happy to get married, but he did insist that his bride be a princess, a true and proper princess. He had travelled the land and met plenty of nice girls who said they were princesses, but none, it seemed to him, were really true and proper princesses. Either their manners were not quite exquisite enough, or their feet were much too big. So he sat in the palace, reading dusty old history books and getting very glum.

One night, there was the most terrible storm. Rain was lashing down, and thunder

and lightning rolled and flashed around the palace. The wind kept blowing out the candles, and everyone huddled closer to the fire. Suddenly there was a great peal from the huge front door bell.

And there, absolutely dripping wet, stood a princess. Well, she said she was a princess, but never did anyone look less like a princess. Her hair was plastered to her head, her dress was wringing wet and her silk

shoes were covered in mud. She was quite alone, without even the smallest maid, and just where had she come from? But she kept insisting she was a princess.

We will see about that, thought the queen. While the dripping girl sat sipping a mug of warm milk and honey, the queen went to supervise the making of the bed in the second-best spare bedroom. She didn't think it necessary to put their late night visitor in the best spare bedroom, after all she might only be a common-or-garden duchess. The queen told the maids to take all the bedclothes and the mattress off the bed. Then she placed one single pea right on the middle of the bedstead. Next the maids piled twenty mattresses on top of the pea, and then twenty feather quilts on top of the mattresses. And so the girl was left for the night.

In the morning, the queen swept into the bedroom in her dressing gown and asked the girl how she had slept.

"I didn't sleep a wink all night." said the girl. "There was a great, hard lump in the middle of the bed. It was quite dreadful. I am sure I am black and blue all over!"

Now everyone knew she really must be a princess, for only a real princess could be as soft-skinned as that. The prince was delighted, and insisted they got married at once, and they lived very happily ever after. They always slept in very soft beds, and the pea was placed in the museum, where it probably still is today.

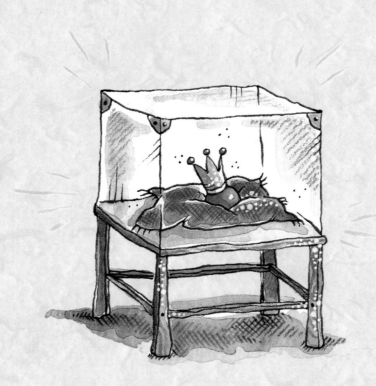

The Mulberry Bush

Here we go round the mulberry bush,
The mulberry bush, the mulberry bush,
Here we go round the mulberry bush,
On a cold and frosty morning.

This is the way we wash our hands,
Wash our hands, wash our hands,
This is the way we wash our hands,
On a cold and frosty morning.

This is the way we wash our clothes,
Wash our clothes, wash our clothes,
This is the way we wash our clothes,
On a cold and frosty morning.

This is the way we go to school,
Go to school, go to school,
This is the way we go to school,
On a cold and frosty morning.

This is the way we come out of school,
Come out of school, come out of school,
This is the way we come out of school,
On a cold and frosty morning.

Join hands and skip round in a circle on the first verse.

This is the chorus.
Mime the actions in the remaining verses.

After each main verse repeat the chorus.

There was an Old Woman

There was an old woman tossed
up in a basket,
Seventeen times as high as the moon;
And where she was going
I couldn't but ask it,
For in her hand she carried a broom.

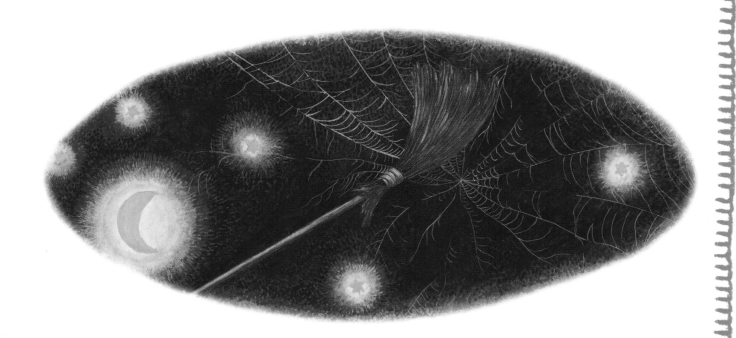

"Old woman, old woman, old woman,"
said I,
"O whither, O whither, O whither
so high?"
"To sweep the cobwebs off the sky!
And I'll be with you by and by."

Monday's Child

Monday's child is fair of face,
Tuesday's child is full of grace,
Wednesday's child is full of woe,
Thursday's child has far to go,

Friday's child is loving and giving,
Saturday's child works hard for a living,
And the child that is born on the
Sabbath day
Is bonny and blithe, and good and gay.

Bye Baby Bunting

Bye baby bunting,
Father's gone a hunting,
To get a little rabbit-skin,
To wrap his little baby in.